JINGLE SMELLS!

By Tex Huntley

Illustrated by MJ Illustrations

Random House 🏠 **New York**

rhcbooks.com

ISBN 978-0-525-58188-8

MANUFACTURED IN CHINA

10 9 8 7 6 5 4 3 2

It was the day before Christmas, and everyone in Adventure Bay had a lot to do. The PAW Patrol was ready to help!

With all the snow on the ground, Mr. Porter couldn't deliver his fresh pumpkin pies. As he was about to call for help, Everest drove by in her plow, clearing the streets so the busy day could begin.

"Ice or snow, I'm ready to go!" she said.

Meanwhile, Rocky helped Mayor Goodway hang stockings over her fireplace.

Ryder, Chase, and Farmer Yumi took
a bale of holiday hay to Bettina.

Over at Katie's Pet Parlor, Marshall and Rubble helped
Katie hang candy canes on her wreath.
"These decorations look great," Marshall said.
"They taste great, too!" said Rubble with his mouth full.

When Rubble was at the Pet Parlor later, he couldn't resist a special extra-soapy holiday bath!

Out at the Seal Island Lighthouse, Zuma helped Cap'n Turbot prepare some seaworthy Christmas treats.

"This superb sweet will be a super surprise for Santa," Cap'n Turbot said as he added a gumball to his gingerbread boat.

Skye found the tallest pine tree to decorate near the Lookout.

"This star will be perfect for the top," she said, zooming through the air.

Down on the ground, Marshall and Chase were busy
stringing their tree with garlands of freshly popped corn.

When they were finished, Ryder relaxed with a cup of hot chocolate while the pups got ready for bed.

"You pups did a good job today," he said. "Now let's get to sleep before Santa visits."

On Christmas morning, the pups woke to find gifts around the tree. Santa had come! There were bouncing balls, brand-new sleds, and best of all . . . tasty pup treats!

"You're all good pups," said Ryder. "Let's have a very merry day!"

The PAW Patrol wishes you a *paw*-some Christmas!